PUFFIN BOOKS

THE WITCH'S DOG AND THE ICE-CREAM WIZARD

Frank Rodgers has written and illustrated a wide range of books for children: picture books, story books, how-to-draw books and a novel for teenagers. His work for Puffin includes the highly popular *Intergalatic Kitchen* series and the picture books *The Bunk-Bed Bus* and *The Pirate and the Pig*, as well as the best-selling *Witch's Dog* titles. He was an art teacher for a number of years before becoming an author and illustrator. He lives in Glasgow with his wife and two children.

D1148513

Frank Rodgers

The Witch's Dog
and the
Ice-Cream Wizard

PUFFIN BOOKS

PUFFIN BOOKS

Published by the Penguin Group
Penguin Books Ltd, 80 Strand, London WC2R 0RL, England
Penguin Putnam Inc., 375 Hudson Street, New York, New York 10014, USA
Penguin Books Australia Ltd, 250 Camberwell Road, Camberwell,
Victoria 3124, Australia
Penguin Books Canada Ltd, 10 Alcorn Avenue, Toronto, Ontario, Canada M4V 3B2
Penguin Books India (P) Ltd, 11 Community Centre, Panchsheel Park,
New Delhi – 110 017, India
Penguin Books (NZ) Ltd, Cnr Rosedale and Airborne Roads, Albany,
Auckland, New Zealand
Penguin Books (South Africa) (Pty) Ltd, 24 Sturdee Avenue,
Rosebank 2196, South Africa

Penguin Books Ltd, Registered Offices: 80 Strand, London WC2R 0RL, England

www.penguin.com

First published 2002
1 3 5 7 9 10 8 6 4 2

Copyright © Frank Rodgers, 2002
All rights reserved

The moral right of the author/illustrator has been asserted

Printed in Hong Kong by Midas Printing Ltd

British Library Cataloguing in Publication Data
A CIP catalogue record for this book is available from the British Library

ISBN 0–141–31222–X

Wilf, the witch's dog, was busy
packing. He and his friends
were going on a school trip.

"Remember to pack your woolly hat and scarf," said Weenie. "It'll be cold up on Snowy Mountain."

Wilf grinned. "I've got my hat and scarf and my gloves," he said. "I can't wait to get to the snow!"

He finished packing and helped
Weenie to make some sandwiches.

Then he took his rucksack outside,
where he met his friends, Harry,
Bertie and Streaky.

They were excited too.
"I'm going to ski downhill as fast as an arrow," boasted Streaky.

"I'm going to zoom down on my snowboard," said Harry.

"I'll probably fall off and slide down on my bottom," said Wilf.

Bertie laughed.
"And I'll pull you all back to the top again," he said.

"Wilf!" called Weenie.
"It's almost
time to go." She
handed him a bag.
"I baked you some cakes,"
she said. "Something tasty to eat
when you get there."

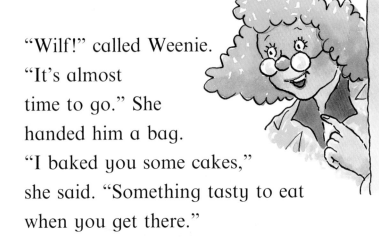

"Thanks," said
Wilf, putting the
bag in his
rucksack.

Just then everyone heard the
tinkling of a bell ...

and round the
corner came a
brightly
coloured cart.

Wilf smiled
with delight
and turned to Weenie.
"How about something tasty to eat
before we go,
Weenie?" he
asked. "Look!
The Ice-Cream
Wizard is here!"

"Good idea, Wilf," said Weenie.
"The Wizard makes the best ice cream in the world.
It's magic and tastes of any flavour you want. Come on, everyone!"

They all dashed out of the garden.

There was already a queue at the
cart, so they waited in line.

"I'm looking forward to my first big
slurp!" said Wilf.
"Me too!" cried Harry, Bertie and
Streaky.

At that moment, Sly Cat and Tricky Toad peered round the corner. They were witches' pets who were jealous of Wilf.

"M-mmmmm," murmured Sly, licking his lips. "The Wizard certainly makes delicious ice cream."

"Delicious ice cream," repeated Tricky eagerly. "Let's join the queue."

"And have to stand behind Wilf?!" snorted Sly. "Never! Anyway," he went on, "we don't have to. Look!" Sly pointed to a wand, which had just fallen out of the Wizard's pocket.

"That's the magic wand the Wizard uses to make his ice cream."

Sly winked at Tricky.
"Finders keepers. We could take it
and make our own ice cream. As
much as we like."
"As much as we like!"
echoed Tricky.

Carefully, Sly crept up behind the Wizard.

Stealthily, he stretched out a hand and snatched the wand.

Quietly, he and Tricky tiptoed away.

When it was Weenie's and Wilf's
turn they stepped up to the counter.

"Five ice-cream cones, please," said
Weenie.

The Ice-Cream Wizard smiled.
"Certainly," he said.
"But could you wait a
moment longer? I've just
run out of ice cream. It
will only take a few
seconds to make
some more."

"Of course
we'll wait,"
said Weenie.

The Wizard took the ingredients
from a shelf.
Into the tub he poured
milk and cream.

Then he added vanilla and sugar.

"All I have to do now," said the Wizard, "is wave my magic wand over the tub. The ingredients will turn into Wizard ice cream!"

He put his hand into his pocket and frowned. "I'm sure I put my wand in there," he muttered, looking round. "Where could it be?"

"Perhaps you dropped it on your way here," suggested Wilf. "We'll help you look for it."

Wilf, Weenie, Harry, Bertie and Streaky searched around the cart and along the lane. But they couldn't see the wand anywhere.

"Oh dear," said the Wizard. "Without my wand I won't be able to make any more ice cream."
"What a shame," said Wilf.

Just then Weenie gasped.
"Wilf! Everyone!" she cried. "I
forgot about the time!
Your class will be
leaving the school
in two minutes!"

"You'd better hurry,"
said the Wizard. "Don't worry
about me. I'll keep on
looking. Thanks for
your help."

"I hope you find your wand!" cried
Wilf. "Come on,
everyone, we'll
have to run!"

"But you won't get to the school in
two minutes even if you do run,"
wailed Weenie. "It's too far."

Wilf thought quickly.
"We'll fly on the magic door,
Weenie!" he cried.

Weenie laughed with relief. "Of
course!" she said. "I'd forgotten. My
front door can fly!"

Quickly she sent
out a spell ...

FLASH!

Weenie's front door
left its hinges ...

and zoomed round the house to
meet them.

"Hop
on, Wilf!"
cried the door.

Wilf and his friends clambered
aboard and held on tightly.

"To the school, please, door," said
Wilf and ...

ZOOM!

the door shot
away at top
speed.

"Bye, Weenie!" called Wilf.

"Bye, Wilf!" cried
Weenie, sniffing.
"See you soon!"

The door sped down the lane ...

swooped over hedges and walls ...

and one minute later it screeched to
a halt at the school gates.

The class was still there.

"Made it!" cried Wilf. "Thanks,
door!"

But then he saw that everyone
looked very glum.

"What's wrong?" he asked.

The head teacher sighed.

"I'm afraid the trip has been cancelled, Wilf," she said. "I've just heard that there's no snow on Snowy Mountain. It's been so warm recently that it has all melted.

"Everything up there is soggy. I'm afraid everyone will have to go back home."

Wilf and his friends turned round
and trudged away, disappointed.
The door floated along beside them.

"Weenie is going to see me sooner
than she thinks," said Wilf.

As they passed a hedge on their way
home they heard a strange sound. It
was a slurping, lip-smacking sort of
sound.

Curious, Wilf and his friends peered
behind the hedge.

There, spooning big dollops of ice
cream into their mouths, were Sly
and Tricky.

On the ground beside them lay the
Wizard's wand.

Wilf glared at them.
"So it was you who
took the wand!" he
cried.

"I might have
guessed!" growled
Bertie. "Pair of
pests!"

"You'd better give
the wand back,"
said Harry.

"Fast!" added
Streaky.

Sly grinned nastily.
"Why don't you give it back, Wilf,"
he said, picking up the wand.

"You're a
dog," he went
on with a
snigger. "So
... fetch!"

And with that, Sly
threw the wand
away as hard as
he could.

Everyone watched as it sailed out of
sight behind a bush.

"Fetch!" tittered Tricky. "That's a
good one, Sly!"
He and Sly went off, laughing, just
as Weenie and the Wizard arrived.

"What are you doing here, Wilf?" cried Weenie in surprise.

Wilf told her everything that had happened.
Weenie and the Wizard were sorry about the cancelled holiday ...
but glad to hear about the wand.

"I just hope it's still in one piece," said the Wizard anxiously.

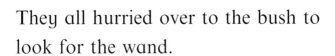

They all hurried over to the bush to look for the wand.

33

Some birds flew away as they approached.

After a few minutes of looking, everyone stopped, puzzled. The wand wasn't there.

"That's funny," said Wilf. "I'm sure this is where Sly threw it."

"Are you certain?" asked the
Wizard.
"Positive," replied Wilf, and his
friends nodded.

"Oh dear," said the
Wizard glumly.
"What will I do
now?!"

"Why don't we have a nice picnic," suggested Weenie. "It'll make us feel better and we might think of something." She pointed up the hill. "There's a lovely view from the top," she said. "Shall we have a look?"

The Wizard sighed again. "Why not," he said.

The magic door gave the Wizard a
lift ... and everyone helped to push
his ice-cream cart up the slope.

At the top, they all
sat down on the grass.
Wilf, Harry, Bertie and Streaky
took out the food for their trip and
shared it round.

As they ate, Wilf looked up into the tree. Birds were flying in and out busily. They had twigs and moss in their beaks. "They're building nests," said Weenie.

"Yes," replied Wilf slowly. "I thought so."

Suddenly he grinned.

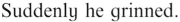

"That's it!" he exclaimed, getting to his feet. "I think I know what happened to the wand!"

He jumped aboard the door. "Up into the tree, please, door," cried Wilf.

"Here we go!"
answered the door,
and rose off the
ground.

"Why are you doing that, Wilf?"
asked Streaky.

"You'll see," Wilf said as he and the
door disappeared among the leaves.

"Be careful,
Wilf!" called
Weenie.
Wilf's voice came
floating back
faintly. "I will ..."

Everyone waited ... and waited.

At last Wilf
appeared again
… and in his
hand he held the wand.
"Hooray!" shouted Weenie
and the Wizard.
"Good for you, Wilf!" cried his
friends.

Wilf smiled as he landed.
"A bird must have mistaken the
wand for a twig," he
said. "I found it stuck
in one of the nests."

The Wizard was overjoyed.
"Now I can make my ice cream again," he said. "And all of you will get the biggest and best ice-cream cones I can make!"
"Brilliant!" everyone cried.

The Wizard waved his wand over the tub ...

FLASH!

and immediately the ingredients
were turned into Wizard Ice Cream.

"Brilliant!"
everyone
cried
again.

Sly and Tricky were
lurking near by and
saw all this.

"They'll all get ice cream now," Sly said to Tricky jealously. He frowned ... then grinned nastily.

"So I'll make sure they get more ice cream than they bargained for!"

Sly aimed a spell at the ice-cream cart ...

45

ZAP!

Suddenly ice cream started to pour out of the tub like lava from a volcano.

It flowed so fast that Wilf and his friends couldn't get out of the way.

46

Just as it was about to cover them,
the magic door sprang into action.

Quick as a flash it flew in front of
them.

The ice cream hit the door instead.
Foaming and bubbling furiously, it
was pushed aside ...

and began to
rush straight at
Sly and Tricky.

"Help!" they
yelped and took
to their heels.

But they
weren't fast
enough.

The ice-cream avalanche poured
over them ...

covering Sly and Tricky from head
to foot in the gooey mess.

"Eurgh!" spluttered Sly as the ice cream got into his ears and went up his nose.

"Yeuk!" wailed Tricky. "I'm all sticky!"

The ice cream stopped flowing and Sly and Tricky got to their feet. Miserably they trudged away through the sweet-smelling sludge.

"I don't think I'll want to eat ice cream ever again," moaned Sly.

"Ever again," echoed Tricky.

"Thanks, door," said Wilf and his
friends.

"Glad to be of help,"
said the door
modestly.

The Wizard looked around him
glumly.

"Oh dear," he said.
"The top of the hill is
covered in ice cream.
What will
we do?"

"I'll have to go home and find a cleaning-up spell in my book of magic," said Weenie.
But Wilf shook his head.
"Don't do that, Weenie," he said and turned to the Wizard.

"Could you make the ice cream cover the whole hill?" he asked.

"I could," replied the Wizard, puzzled. "But why?"

"Yes, why, Wilf?" asked Weenie.

"You'll see," said Wilf mysteriously. "You'll see."

The Wizard waved his wand and …

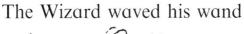

FLASH!

the ice cream spread out like a white
blanket over the entire hill.

"Thank you," said Wilf to the Wizard.
"But now what?" asked Bertie. "It's
starting to melt already."

"Watch," said
Wilf.

Shutting his eyes, he concentrated
hard and ...

ZIIIIP!

sent out a super-strong
freeze spell.

Suddenly the whole hill was covered
in sparkling, *frozen* ice
cream.

It was just like snow!

"Wilf! You're a genius!"
cried Weenie. "I see what
you're up to. Now everyone
can have their snowy holiday!"

Wilf grinned.
"That's right," he
said.

"Yippeeee!" yelled Harry, Bertie and
Streaky.

56

Streaky
rushed off to
tell everyone.

Harry made little
flags to mark out the
ski runs ...

and Bertie collected all the skis,
snowboards and sledges from the
school.

Half an hour later the hill was full
of happy holidaymakers.

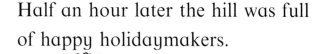

"Well
done, Wilf!"
shouted Weenie
and the head
teacher as they
sped past.

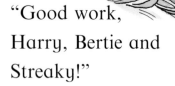

"Good work,
Harry, Bertie and
Streaky!"

"And hooray for
the Ice-Cream
Wizard!" cried the
witches' pets.

SLURP!

The Wizard beamed as he gave
Wilf, Harry, Bertie and Streaky the
biggest ice-cream cones they had
ever seen.

"Thanks!"
they said.

As the magic door began to slide
down the hill Wilf and his friends
took their first lick.

The Wizard laughed because it was
the noisiest one he had ever heard.